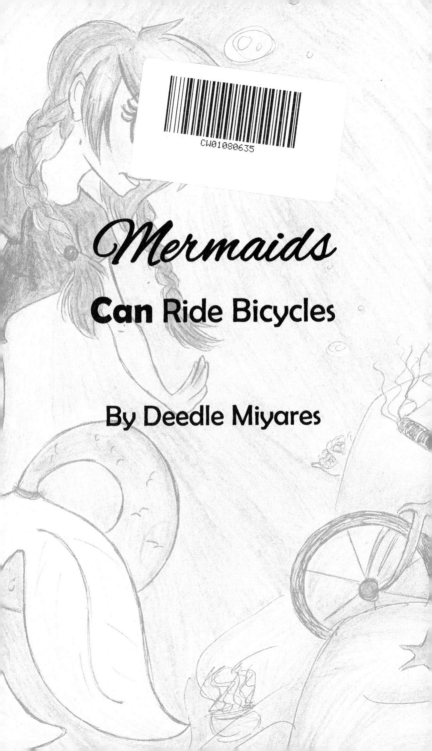

# *Mermaids*

## **Can** Ride Bicycles

By Deedle Miyares

## Chapter One

Hi. My name is Meredith. Everyone calls me Mer. I'm six and three-quarters years old. I like being six and three-quarters because it means I get to have my birthday soon.

I love my mom, dad, and brother. My brother's name is Doug. He is big. He just turned ten and has two numbers in his age. One and zero. Sometimes I can't wait to be big. Being little means you can't always do what you want. Mom says that is true when you are big, too, but I think she is just being silly.

We live in a neighborhood with a park and my school. It is fun being close to the park. Now that my brother is big, we can even go to school by ourselves. That makes me feel big, too.

Our neighborhood probably looks like one you have seen before. It might even look like yours. There is one way I know it is not like yours. My house is in the ocean.

That probably sounds like I am playing pretend, but it is true. I live in the ocean. Not on the ocean in a boat. In the ocean, way down deep. I can do this because I am a mermaid.

I am a mermaid because I am a girl. My brother and dad are mermen because they are boys. We are all merfolk, and we live in the ocean all the time. I love being a mermaid.

Merfolk look a lot like people. Some have dark hair. Some have light hair. Some have blue eyes and others have brown.

I have long, brown hair. I like to wear my hair in two braids and feel them flow behind me in the water. My eyes are blue. I like to wear purple best of all, but I wear all kinds of colors.

One thing about me is very different from you. I have a fin instead of legs. I love my fin. It lets me swim really fast.

I may be little, but sometimes I can beat my brother in a race. Most of the time he wins. Sometimes I think he lets me win because I am small. He is a nice brother and likes to make me smile.

He is even nice to my best friend. Her name is Delilah. She lives in the house next door. We have a lot in common. That means there are things about us that are the same.

We both like to play with our dolls. We both like to draw pictures. We both like to make and invent things. We even have the same color hair. Sometimes merfolk ask us if we are sisters, and we just laugh.

Last week, Delilah and I made the most amazing invention. It was not a brand new invention. It was already made, but we made it better. Want to hear about my bicycle?

## Chapter Two

Last week, Delilah and I went to the park. My brother Doug came with us because we are only six years old and he is ten. I am lucky to have an older brother who will take me places. If I was the older one, I would have to wait until I was ten.

Delilah and I wanted to race. Our backyard is not very big, and we wanted a long race.

"Mom. Can Delilah and I go to the park to race?" I asked. The park is across the reef from our house. If my mom looks out the front window, she can watch us race.

"I am cooking dinner right now. Maybe when I am done," Mom said.

"We can go with them," Doug offered.

Doug had his friend Marc over to play. Marc was even older than Doug. He just turned eleven. Eleven is made with two ones. I like that because it is the same forward and backward. He is Delilah's brother.

"You can see us from the window," Delilah added.

"Did you ask your mom, Delilah?" my mom asked.

Delilah shook her head, no.

"I will call your mom, then, and if she says it is fine, you all can go." My mom was friends with Delilah's mom, and they even called each other by their first names. I call Delilah's mom Ms. Ann, but my mom just calls her

Ann.

My mom talked to Ms. Ann, and she said yes. My mom had us all promise to stay together and to make sure we could see each other.

"Race you!" I shouted and swam out the front door. Everyone followed, and even though I was fast, Doug got there before any of us did.

"I won!" Doug sounded very proud.

"Want to race with us?" I asked him. I hoped that next time I would win.

"Naw," Doug answered. "I see some kids from school."

"It looks like they are going to play kickball," Marc said. Marc is a really good kickball player. He can hit the ball with his fin and make it go so far that he always gets to a base. Sometimes he even gets all the way around and scores a point.

Some of the kids from school were waving them over, and the boys swam to the kickball field. Delilah and I decided we would just race alone.

## Chapter Three

"Should we have silly races?" Delilah asked.

Delilah and I loved silly races. Sometimes we raced backward. Sometimes we raced spinning as we swam. Sometimes we got extra silly and tried to see who could go the slowest.

"Hmmm," I said. "Maybe we could do a zigzag race?"

Zigzag races were super fun. We would swim side to side on our way to the finish line. If we ended up in the center at the same time, we gave each other a high five and laughed.

"Zigzag racing it is," Delilah said. She sounded excited.

"On your mark. Get set. Go!" I yelled, and off we went. Back and forth and meeting in the middle almost every time.

We were almost halfway to the finish line when the kickball bounced in front of us and flew to the left. I looked over to the kickball field. It looked like Marc was the one who kicked it. He was swimming around the bases and everyone was clapping.

"We should get the ball," I said. I forgot all about the race.

We swam over to where we saw it fly. It went really far. This part of the park was great for a leisurely swim, but not really for playing games, so we didn't come here often.

The turquoise ball was the same color as

some of the plants. That made it hard to see. We looked and looked. Finally, I found it wedged into the coral and yanked it hard.

I pulled so hard I fell backward as the ball came out. I bumped into my brother. Delilah laughed.

"I didn't know you were here, Doug," I said. He was rubbing his fin. "Sorry I bumped you."

"No worries, Mer." Doug gave me a hug. "It was an accident."

I handed him the ball, and he swam back to his friends. A little catfish caught my attention. I want a catfish, but my mom always says no. Mom thinks pets are hard work. I think they are cute.

I reached to pet the catfish, but he swam away. Delilah followed the cute little fish. I went with her. Maybe we would be lucky and he would play with us.

## Chapter Four

We had almost caught up to the catfish when I saw something shiny in the coral. At first, I thought it was a piece of sea glass. Sometimes pieces of glass end up in the water. It takes a long time, but the water makes them smooth and pretty.

I went to grab the sea glass, but it wasn't glass. It was metal. It was not small, either. I pulled it out of the coral.

The metal was beautiful. It was pink with sparkles. It had a seat, and on the side it said B-I-C-Y-C-L-E. I had seen that word before in a book but had never seen an actual bicycle.

20

You probably have a bicycle, but merfolk don't. We swim most places. So when I saw that word on the side, I got very excited.

"This is a bicycle," I said in awe. I pointed to the letters one at a time. B-I-C-Y-C-L-E."

"Wow!" Delilah said. She ran her fingers over the letters. "It is so pretty."

"I love the way it sparkles," I replied.

"Do you know how it works?" she asked.

I knew that bicycles had a seat and got you from one place to another. I knew that I liked them. What I didn't know was how to use one.

"I don't," I said.

"What should we do with it?" Delilah asked.

"I think we should get my brother and take it home," I answered. "Maybe my dad knows what to do with it."

She agreed. When we got to Doug, the game was already over. Doug and Marc swam over, looking the bicycle up and down carefully, smiles on their faces. Neither one of them had ever seen one either.

I really hoped Dad was home from work. He knew about all kinds of things. I was sure he could help us figure out the shiny pink bicycle.

## Chapter Five

Dad was in the front yard and had a huge smile on his face. In his hand was his lunch bag. He had just gotten home from work.

"Hello, kids," my dad said. "What do you have there?"

"Mer and Delilah found it at the park. It's a bicycle," Doug answered.

"It's from humans," Marc added. Marc loves finding things from humans. He says he wants to be an anthropologist when he grows up. That is a big word meaning he wants to learn about other merfolk and people.

"I see that," my dad said. He knelt down

24

by the bicycle. "I think we should take this into the garage and see what we can learn about it."

We followed my dad into the garage.

It was easy to move the bicycle because it had wheels and rolled on the ground. I learned in school that humans use wheels for a lot of different things. They seemed pretty handy.

Dad turned on the light, and we stood around the bicycle. Dad looked it over. First, he looked at what he called handlebars. They had fun ribbons on the end that moved with the current. I bet they would look nice if Delilah and I braided them. The ribbons were purple, which was one of my favorite colors.

"Dad, have you ever seen a real life bicycle before?" I asked as he played with the wheels.

"No, Mer," he said as he turned a flat piece that made the wheels move. "I have seen them in books, though. These are called pedals. They make the wheels move."

"Did the books tell you how people use them? You know, to make them go?" Marc asked.

Dad shook his head, no.

"I want to ride it," I announced. "I know bicycles help people move from one place to another. Can you show me how?"

"Merfolk can't ride bicycles," Dad said.

"Mom told me I can do anything I put my heart into," I answered. "I am going to ride this bicycle."

"Mom is always right," Doug said.

"She is always right," Dad said with a smile. "I don't know how you can ride it, though." Dad scratched his chin.

"We could go to the library and look it up," Delilah suggested.

"Yes!" I said and gave her a high five.

"Dinner!" Mom called from the house.

"Tomorrow?" I asked Delilah.

"Tomorrow," she agreed. "We have to go home for dinner, too."

Marc and Delilah swam home, and we went inside to eat dinner. We would learn more about bicycles in the morning. The library is a great place to learn things. I could hardly wait.

## Chapter Six

I woke up bright and early the next day. I was so excited to learn more about the bicycle. I hoped that Delilah would get there soon.

"Mer, breakfast," my mom called.

"Coming," I called back. I grabbed my backpack, a notebook, and some pens before heading into the kitchen.

If I was going to read about bicycles, I might need things to take notes. My teacher says it is good to write new things down when you are doing research. Research is the big word she uses for trying to find out about new things. Today, I hoped to learn a lot of

29

new things about my bicycle.

"I'm here, Mom," I said as I swam into the kitchen.

"I see you are ready for your research," my mom said with a smile. My mom loves to learn things. She says learning is fun. I think she is right.

I sat at the table. "Today I want to learn how to ride a bicycle. Dad said that mermaids can't ride bicycles."

That made me sad because I really wanted to learn how.

Mom handed me some breakfast. It smelled yummy.

"Thanks, Mom." I took a bite. It was *really* yummy. "I told Dad that I could do anything I put my heart into."

"It is true, Mer. You can." Mom was

smiling.

"That's what Dad said after I told him that," I answered.

I ate my breakfast and waited for Delilah. It was still early in the morning, and the library wasn't even open yet. I was anxious to go and figure out how to ride the human machine.

"Mer, sweetie," Mom said.

"Yes, Mom?" I answered.

"Maybe you should go to the garage and draw your bicycle. That way you have it with you when you are in the library," she suggested.

"That is a great idea, Mom," I said before swimming to the garage. I drew it from all sides. By the time Delilah got there, I had five drawings done.

"Those look really good," Delilah complimented me. Compliment is a big word that means that she was telling me I did a good job. Compliments always make me smile.

"Thank you," I said and put on my backpack. "It was Mom's idea. She said it will help us at the library."

"Is she taking us to the library or should I ask my mom?" Delilah asked.

"My mom said she would. She likes the library even more than we do," I answered.

"Let's ask if we can leave now," Delilah said. "My mom says I have to be home by lunch."

"Sounds good to me," I answered. "I have wanted to go since before it was time to wake up."

I was so excited. I was going to ride a bicycle. I was determined to prove that mermaids can ride bicycles.

## Chapter Seven

The library was just opening when we got there. Mom told us to take our time.

We swam up to the librarian's desk.

"Hello, Mrs. Finn," Delilah and I said at the same time. That made us giggle.

"Well hello, girls. What can I help you with today? Books about catfish again?" Mrs. Finn asked.

"Not today, Mrs. Finn. Today we want to learn about bicycles," I said in my best researcher voice.

"We found one at the park yesterday," Delilah added.

Mrs. Finn put her finger on her cheek. She did that a lot when she was thinking. "Hmmmm," she said but kept thinking. "Can you describe it?"

"I can do better than that," I answered.

I pulled out my notebook and showed her the pictures I had drawn.

"These are very detailed, Mer. Nice job," Mrs. Finn complimented. "I think if we look over on the back shelf near the window, we can find the books you need."

Mrs. Finn led the way, and we followed her.

"I think this shelf is your best bet," Mrs. Finn said. "What are you hoping to find?"

"We are going to ride this bicycle," I told her.

"Oh, sweet girl, mermaids can't ride

bicycles," Mrs. Finn said before leaving.

"She is wrong," I told Delilah. "We can do anything we put our hearts into."

"Yes, we can. Let's find the books we need," Delilah agreed.

We looked and looked through the books on the shelf. They were filled with stories about humans. Some of them had a lot of pictures. Those were the books I was looking for. I wanted to see how they rode these bicycles, so I could do it, too.

"I found one," Delilah exclaimed.

"You did?" I said too loudly.

Someone said, "Shh," and we stopped talking. The picture was perfect. It had a bunch of kids my age wearing hats on their heads and sitting on their bicycles. The picture labeled the hats as *helmets* and the bicycles as *bikes*.

"Oh, no," I said very quietly so we didn't get in trouble. "Look here."

I pointed to the picture on the page. It looked like each kid had one foot on each of the flat pieces.

"See how each of their feet are on these pieces?" I asked.

"The ones labeled *pedals*?" she asked in reply.

"Yes, those." I finally saw why merfolk said that mermaids can't ride bicycles. "We only have one fin."

"So we really can't ride bicycles?" Delilah asked. She sounded sad.

"No, we can do anything we put our hearts into," I answered. "The question is, how?"

## Chapter Eight

We looked at lots and lots of books. Being a good researcher, I drew lots of pictures in my notebook. Delilah did, too.

By the time we got home, I finally had an idea. It was more than an idea. It was a plan. I was going to fix the bicycle so I could ride it.

Delilah got home just in time for lunch. She and her mom had errands to run, so she wasn't going to be able to help me with the plan. My mom told me that was okay because I needed to eat lunch first and clean my room.

I liked lunch, but I didn't like cleaning my room. It took me forever to clean my room.

My mom said it was only an hour.

"Mom, is Dad going to be home soon?" I asked.

"Probably in another hour. Why, Mer?" she asked.

"I was hoping to use some of his tools and things in the garage," I said.

"Would you like to call him?" Mom offered.

"Thanks, Mom. That would be great." I gave her a hug.

I talked to Dad, and he said I could use the things I needed. I just had to promise to ask Doug to help me since some things were for big merpeople. He made me promise to be very careful. I promised and told him I would see him soon.

"Doug!" I shouted. Mom did not look

pleased. She says we should swim into the room people are in instead of shouting.

"What's up, Mer?" Doug swam into the kitchen.

"Want to help me in the garage?" I crossed my fingers for luck as I asked. I really wanted him to help me.

"Maybe. What are you doing?" he asked.

I showed him my sketches, and he smiled.

"That is a great plan, sis. I would love to help you."

We went into the garage and pulled out all of the things we needed. We cut, nailed, glued, and sanded. It was starting to look like my picture.

A couple of times things were not as easy as I thought they would be. Especially holding things straight while trying to nail them together. Doug helped a lot with those things. He is a really good big brother.

"I think this is going to work," he said when we were just about done.

"I hope so. If it does, you can ride it, too," I said. He was probably a bit too tall for it. It would still be fun, though.

"I was hoping you would let me. I never heard of a merman riding a bicycle," he said as he turned the front wheel. "It looks really good." He looked proud.

"Yes it does," my dad said. He startled us! I hadn't heard him come home.

"Hey, Dad." I swam over and gave him a hug. "Did you just get home?"

"I did just a few minutes ago. Your mom asked me to get you both for dinner," he said.

"But I want to try the bicycle," Doug said.

44

He sounded disappointed.

"Me, too," I pouted.

"Me, three," my dad joined in. "But it is time for dinner. During dinner, you can tell me all about your new machine. Mom told me that humans have two words for bicycles."

"They do, Dad. They also call them bikes." I beamed up at him. "And humans wear hats on their heads called helmets. They help protect their heads if they fall when they are riding the bikes."

"What else did you learn today?" Dad asked as we swam into the house for dinner.

I told him all about the things I learned at the library with Delilah and all the things Doug and I did in the garage. He told me he was very proud. It made me happy.

I was hoping to ride the bicycle after

dinner, but Mom told us we should wait until the morning. She was right. Trying something new like that in the dark was not the best idea. It still was not what I wanted to hear.

I called Delilah and told her about all the things Doug and I were able to do with the bicycle. She told me she was sure it would work.

I promised her I would wait until she came over in the morning to try it. She told me she was bringing Marc. He was hoping to try it, too.

It was hard for me to fall asleep. I was too excited. I decided I should write a story instead. I wrote a story about a mermaid who could ride a bicycle. I even drew the illustrations.

It was a fiction story. That means it was

make believe. I hoped in the morning I could write a second story. This one was going to be called *How I Rode a Bicycle,* and it was going to be true.

## Chapter Nine

Today was the day. Today I was going to ride the bicycle. I wanted to do somersaults, I was so excited.

Delilah and Marc showed up right after breakfast. They seemed just as excited as me. Mom made us wait until she and Dad could come outside. They wanted to see the first time a mermaid rode a bicycle.

"I want to see!" Marc said.

"Be patient," I answered. I sounded like my mom, and it made me giggle.

Delilah asked, "Does it look just like the pictures we drew yesterday?"

48

"Almost." I pointed to Doug. "He helped me fix a few things, but it looks mostly the same."

"It was a really good design," Doug said. "I think it will work."

Doug gave me a high five.

My mom and dad finally came out, and we opened the garage door. Dad's eyes opened wide and he smiled. I could see he was proud of my design.

"I think that will work," Dad said.

"I agree," Mom said.

I pushed the bicycle out of the garage. I was a bit scared. What if it didn't work? What if mermaids really couldn't ride bicycles?

"Mer, if it doesn't work, you can try again," Mom said. "Mermaids can do anything they put their hearts into."

Mom made me feel brave, and I sat on the seat of the bicycle. I put my fin where we built our platform. I pushed down and then pulled up. I repeated it over and over.

"It is working!" Delilah shouted.

"It is!" Mark agreed.

Doug and Dad clapped and mom whistled. I had really done it. I was a mermaid. I was riding a bicycle. Mermaids *could* ride bicycles!

We spent the morning taking turns. It turned out that riding a bicycle was really fun. Dad looked a little silly on the bicycle because he was so tall. He was able to go really fast, though, and we all gave him high fives.

"I knew you could do it," Mom said after giving me a hug. "Mermaids can do anything they put their hearts into."

"I know, Mom," I said. "Mermaids can ride bicycles."

## About the Authors

Deedle loves to read, write, and listen to stories. *Mermaids Can Ride Bicycles* was a story originally told by Deedle when she was five-years-old. She loves unicorns, mermaids, and all things fairy. She lives in Michigan with the rest of the Miyares clan.

Printed in Great Britain
by Amazon

23419308R00031